W9-BNV-532

ONLY ONE HERO CAN PREVENT PROBLEMS LIKE THIS AT JURASSIC WORLD—OWEN! BUILD HIS MINIFIGURE AND TURN THE PAGE TO LEARN MORE ABOUT WHAT HE DOES AT THE PARK.

OWEN GRADY

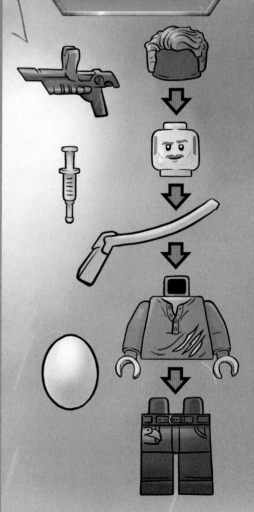

OWEN IS LOOKING FOR RAPTOR EGGS THAT FELL OUT OF A HELICOPTER WHEN IT CRASHED. CAN YOU SPOT NINE OF THEM IN THE PICTURE?

OWEN HAS DELIVERED THE DINOSAUR EGGS TO THE LAB. LOOK AT THE SEQUENCES AND COLOR IN THE BLANK EGGS IN EACH ROW THE RIGHT COLOR.

WHO OR WHAT CAN OWEN SEE WITH HIS TORCH?

WHEN OWEN WAS FEEDING LITTLE RAPTORS, THE SCENT OF THE MEAT ATTRACTED AN UNINVITED GUEST! CONNECT THE DOTS TO SEE WHO IT WAS, THEN COLOR IN THE PICTURE.

THESE PARK WORKERS NEED TO TRACK DOWN A MISSING DINOSAUR. CONNECT THEM WITH THEIR GADGETS BY FINDING PAIRS OF THE SAME COLOR SEQUENCES IN THE BOXES.

OWEN IS LOOKING FOR AN ESCAPED DINOSAUR. MAYBE YOU CAN FIND THE NAME T. REX FIRST IN THE GRID?

O	R	A	W	Z	O	W
E	O	W	E	N	B	T
Z	M	E	B	O	M	R
W	O	W	E	Z	O	E
A	E	A	R	E	W	X
O	W	E	N	M	E	O
M	E	O	Z	W	N	B

CIRCLE THE FOUR THINGS THAT OWEN WILL NEED FOR HIS JUNGLE EXPEDITION.

ONLY ONE OF THE RAPTORS HAS HER TWIN ON THE PAGE. DRAW A LINE TO CONNECT THE SISTERS.

WHICH OF THE SQUARES WILL COMPLETE THIS DINOSAUR'S PORTRAIT?

A

B

C

D

SEARCH FOR *BRACHIOSAURUS*

YOU'RE NEW HERE! I'LL SHOW YOU AROUND THE PARK. ONE OF THE BIGGEST AND MOST WELL-KNOWN HERBIVOROUS DINOSAURS SHOULD BE SOMEWHERE NEARBY.

THE BRACHIOSAURUS MUST BE HERE SOMEWHERE!

I READ THIS DINO'S AS LONG AS THREE SCHOOL BUSES. HOW CAN WE NOT FIND HER?

WELL . . . YES SHE IS . . . BUT SHE ALSO KNOWS HOW TO . . . UMMM . . . HIDE.

THE END

HELP OWEN UNTANGLE THE LINES TO FIND
OUT THE NAMES OF THE DINOSAURS.

BRACHIOSAURUS

VELOCIRAPTOR

PTERANODON

T. REX

DILOPHOSAURUS

STYGIMOLOCH

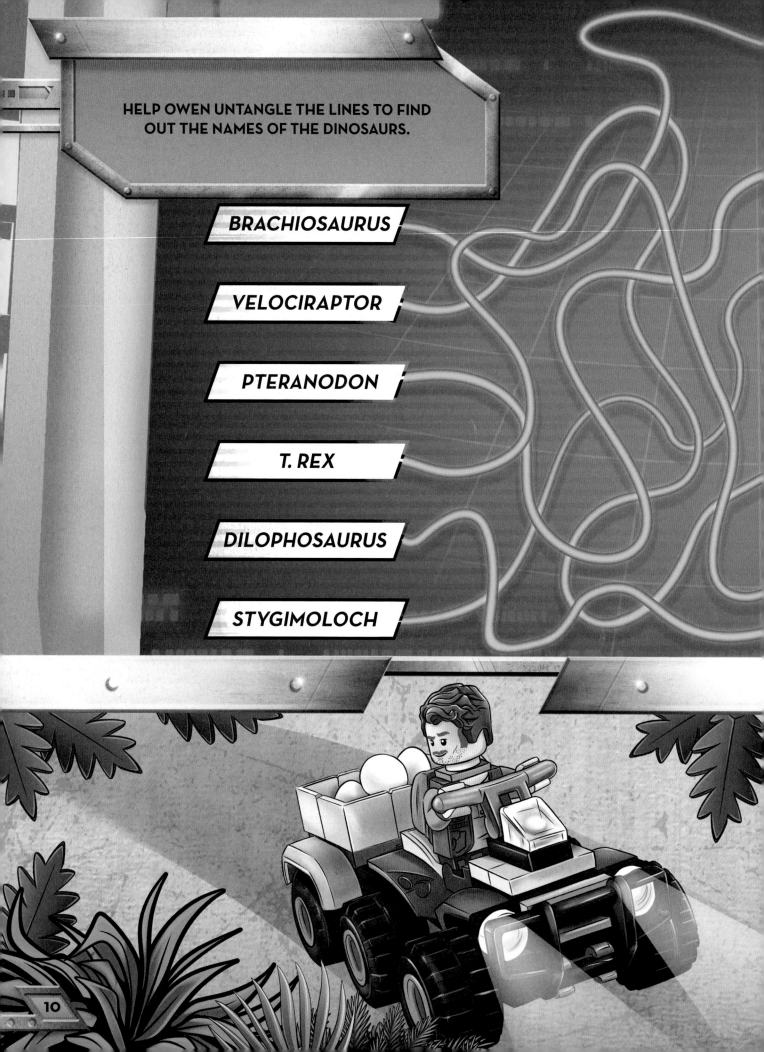

OWEN NEEDS TO KNOW HOW THE VEHICLES
HE USES ARE CONSTRUCTED. HELP HIM BY CIRCLING
THE BRICKS THAT AREN'T FROM HIS QUAD BIKE.

CLAIRE AND THE GUARDS ARE TRYING
TO CATCH A RUNAWAY PTERANODON.
DRAW LINES BETWEEN EACH OF THE PAIRS
OF LETTERS TO MAKE A NET.

CIRCLE THE DINOSAUR THAT
IS IDENTICAL TO THE ONE
IN THE BIG IMAGE.

WHICH DINOSAUR ARE OWEN AND CLAIRE TRACKING? GET THROUGH THE MAZE TO FIND OUT.

TRICERATOPS

T. REX

STIGGY

STIGGY IS ON THE RUN AND OWEN'S NOT HERE!
FIND THE PIECE BELOW THAT DOES NOT MATCH
THE PICTURE AND HOPEFULLY OWEN
WILL TURN UP.

OWEN IS GOING INTO ACTION.
DESIGN AN AWESOME DINOSAUR
TRAP HE CAN USE.

THIS EXACT SEQUENCE OF DINOSAURS ONLY APPEARS ONCE IN THE GRID. CAN YOU SEE WHERE IT IS?

TRAINING A RAPTOR

THE END

OWEN IS FOLLOWING THE T. REX AS SHE HEADS OFF ON A NIGHTTIME HUNT. WHICH SHADOW IS HERS?

DRAW A PAIR OF GOGGLES FOR OWEN SO HE CAN SEE THE DINOSAUR AT NIGHT.

HA! THERE SHE IS!

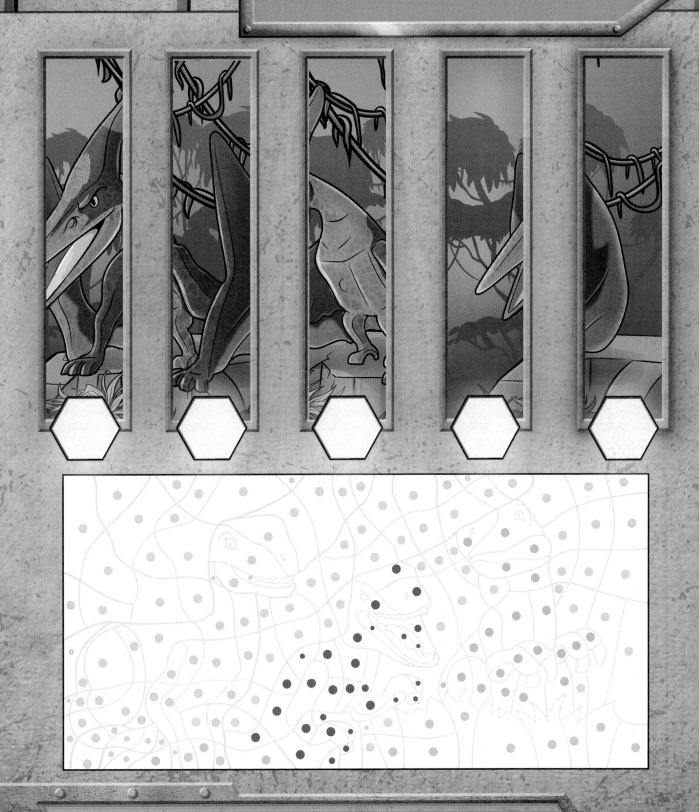

CLAIRE'S CAMERA BROKE AND THE PICTURES ARE IN PIECES. LOOK AT THE MIXED UP DINOSAUR PICTURE PIECES. NUMBER THEM TO PUT THEM IN THE CORRECT ORDER.

COLOR IN THE SHAPES THE SAME COLOR AS THE SPOTS TO REVEAL THE DINOSAURS.

OWEN IS FOLLOWING THE T. REX. LEAD HIM TO THE RUNAWAY DINOSAUR BY STEPPING ALONG A PATH OF TYRANNOSAURUS PICTURES.

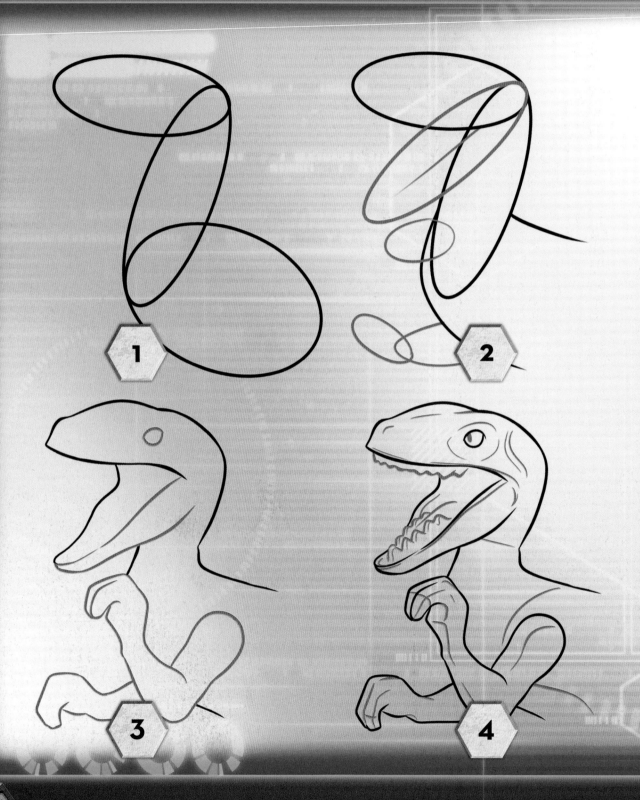

PRACTICE DRAWING IT HERE.

THERE IS ONE MISTAKE ON EACH
OF THESE PORTRAITS OF OWEN.
CAN YOU SPOT THEM ALL?

"ALL ABOUT ME" BY OWEN GRADY

I'VE JUST STARTED WORKING AT JURASSIC WORLD, WHICH IS THE GREATEST PLACE ON EARTH! THERE'S ALWAYS SOMETHING GOING ON.

I USED TO BE IN THE MARINES BUT NOW I WORK AS AN ANIMAL BEHAVIORIST. I CAN COMMUNICATE WITH ANY ANIMAL!

I'M A VERY GOOD MOTORCYCLIST—WHICH COMES IN HANDY WHEN WORKING WITH DINOSAURS.

I'M VERY FAST, WHICH IS ALSO IMPORTANT FOR A JURASSIC WORLD WORKER.

I'M AN INCREDIBLE TRACKER.

THEY'VE GOTTA BE AROUND HERE SOMEWHERE, RIGHT?

6

AND I'M FAMOUS FOR MY GREAT IDEAS.

7

THIS MIGHT SOUND LIKE I'M BRAGGING, BUT WHENEVER SOMETHING BAD HAPPENS IN THE PARK I HEAR . . .

I NEED TO INVENT A NEW ATTRACTION FOR MY PARK.

MAYBE I COULD TRY TRAINING SOME VELOCIRAPTORS?

AND THEN I KNOW IT'S TIME FOR ME TO STEP IN.

OWEN!!!

OWEN IS HIDING SOMEWHERE IN THE PICTURE, WATCHING THE DINOSAURS. CAN YOU SPOT HIM AND ALL THE CREATURES HE IS SPYING ON?

THE FOURTH RAPTOR IS ABOUT TO HATCH, BUT OWEN LOST THE EGG! HELP HIM FIND IT, QUICK!

DRAW LINES TO CONNECT THE MISSING DINOSAUR PARTS WITH THE CORRECT DINOSAURS AND COLOR THEM IN.

A NEW BATCH OF DINOSAURS HAS ARRIVED ON THE ISLAND, BUT DR. WU IS HAVING PROBLEMS COUNTING THEM. HOW MANY LITTLE RAPTORS ARE THERE?

COLOR THE DINOSAUR THAT DOESN'T BELONG TO THE GROUP.

ANSWERS

ANSWERS

14

16-17

20

21

22-23

25

28

29

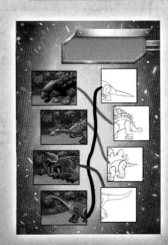

30

20